*For Mary Emmons
and all her friends-and-relations*

Puffin Books, Penguin Books Ltd, Harmondsworth, Middlesex, England
Viking Penguin Inc., 40 West 23rd Street, New York, New York 10010, U.S.A.
Penguin Books Australia Ltd, Ringwood, Victoria, Australia
Penguin Books Canada Limited, 2801 John Street, Markham, Ontario, Canada L3R 1B4
Penguin Books (N.Z.) Ltd, 182-190 Wairau Road, Auckland 10, New Zealand

Puffin/Moonlight
First published by Collins Publishers Ltd, 1975
Text copyright © Georgess McHargue, 1975
Illustrations copyright © Michael Foreman, 1975
Published in Pocket Puffins in 1988 in association with Moonlight Publishing Ltd,
131 Kensington Church Street, London W8

Printed in Italy by La Editoriale Libraria

PRIVATE ZOO

Written by Georgess McHargue
Illustrated by Michael Foreman

POCKET  PUFFINS

Lewis Harvey wanted to go to the zoo. He had a big book with pictures of animals.

Sometimes he saw animals on television.
But Lewis wanted to see them *alive*.

Lewis had a big family and lots of
friends.
You'd think one of them would have
been *glad* to take Lewis to the zoo.
They weren't. They said:

"It's too hot."

"It's too col

t's too far."

"You're too little."

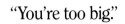

"My feet hurt."
(That was Lewis's Uncle Oscar.)

Lewis looked at his Uncle Oscar. He was all fat and smiley and smooth, with little twinkly eyes.
"Oh, my," said Lewis to himself.

Lewis was deeply disappointed. He *did* want to go to the zoo.
He especially wanted to see the hippopotamus, all fat and smiley and smooth, with little eyes.

Lewis went into the living room.
There were his brother and sister,
building a model spaceship.
They were very good at putting things
together, but not so good at cleaning
up afterwards.
"Goodness me," thought Lewis.

In the kitchen, bony Aunt Joyce was singing as she washed some carrots. His mother was carefully tasting the spaghetti.
Lewis smiled. "I think I'll go for a walk," he said.

Cathy and Carrie Elling were playing hopscotch with Lewis's sister May. Thunk, thunk, thunk, went their feet.

"Do you want to play?" asked Carrie.
"No, thanks," answered Lewis. "I'll just
watch."

From an upstairs window of the building next door, old Mr Hooton put his thin hands on the sill and leaned out to look at the world.
Lewis could see his big round glasses gleaming. "Don't fall out of the tree," said Lewis, very quietly to himself.

Down the block Lewis stretched up to
look through the hole in the fence
where the new supermarket was going
to be.
He thought that was even better than
the zoo.

At his vegetable stand on the corner
Mr Mackey was shuffling about in his
baggy trousers, whisking the flies away
from the fruit.
Lewis wished he had some peanuts to
offer him.

Just as Lewis came by, Fred and Ed
Bruno started a fight in front of the
delicatessen.
They wrestled and rolled until big
Mr Bruno came out and stopped them.

"Just look at Lewis, minding his own business," said Mr Bruno.
"Why can't you boys be like him?"
Fred and Ed stuck their tongues out at Lewis.

Lewis saw his tall cousin Charles
coming towards him.
He started to say hello,
but Charles didn't even see him.

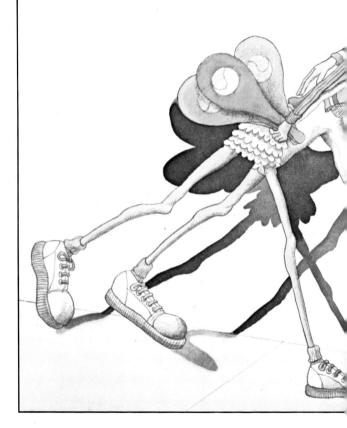

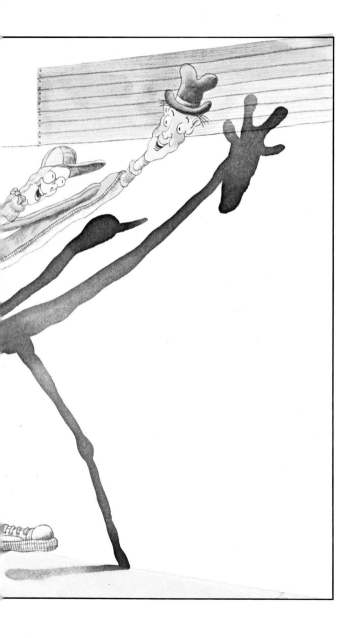

Lewis went into the sweet shop and bought some sour balls from Mrs Humpmeyer, who never smiled. Lewis's father always said it was because she had indigestion.

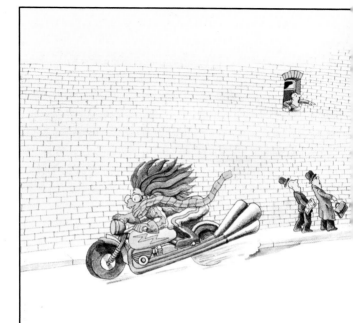

Lewis decided he had walked far
enough.
On his way back he saw Sally Hyme's
brother charge down the street on his
motorcycle. Lewis wished his skate-
board would roar like that.

Next came Jeanie Hayes running towards the park in her striped jersey.

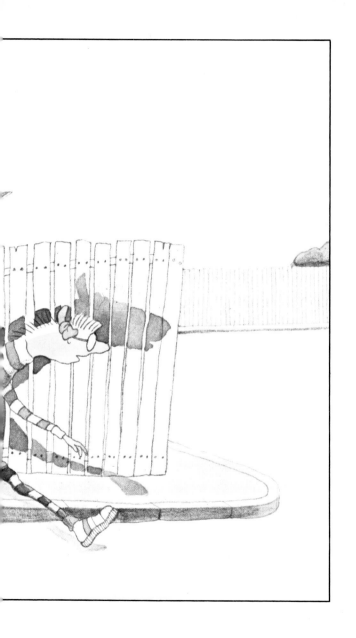

Lewis saw that Arthur Farnum was cleaning out his cellar again.

He got so interested watching that he was almost knocked down by four big boys he didn't know. They were playin football.

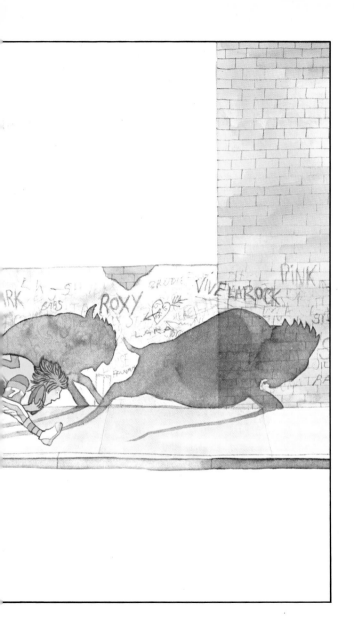

Lewis was glad to get home.

He had had quite an afternoon.

On the stairs he met Mrs Muldoon,
who lived next door.
"I'm taking Ben and Mike to the zoo
tomorrow, Lewis," she said.
"Would you like to come?"
Lewis smiled nicely at Mrs Muldoon.
"No, thank you, Mrs Muldoon,"
he said.
"I've just *been* to the zoo."

GEORGESS McHARGUE is American and lives in Cambridge, Massachusetts, in the United States. It was the mixture of every race, every colour, every shape, in crowded, cosmopolitan New York, which inspired this book. She received the American Best Children's Book Award in 1977.

MICHAEL FOREMAN has illustrated well over fifty children's books. As well as the books he has written himself (including, of course, *Panda's Puzzle*, already published in **Pocket Puffins**), he has also illustrated the works of such authors as Charles Dickens, Hans Christian Andersen, the Brothers Grimm, Roald Dahl, J.M. Barrie, Shakespeare ... and Terry Jones. His work has won most of the sought-after awards for illustration, including the Kate Greenaway Medal, the Francis Williams Prize, for which he is now a judge, the Kurt Maschler Award and the Bologna Graphic Prize. Ideas for his own stories are very often supplied by his two youngest sons, Ben and Jack.

SHADOW PLAYS

You can do a lot with shadows.

In Java, in the Far East, they used to make plays using only puppets which cast their shadows on a screen.

Sometimes boxers use their own shadows to fight against to help train themselves to move fast.

Shadows can be used to make portraits. The portraitist draws or cuts round the sitter's shadow cast on a piece of paper. These portraits are called 'silhouettes.'

And you can make your own stories with shadows. Look at the pictures opposite, and then make these shadows, and others, by placing your hands between a blank wall and a bright light. Perhaps you could make the dog bark?

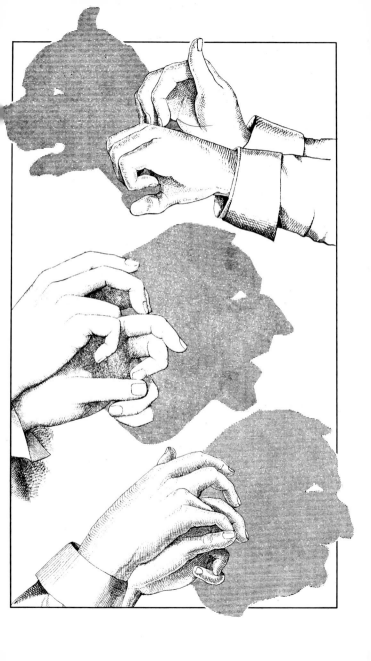

More Pocket Puffins for you to enjoy!

Picture books for the early reader

Billy Goat and His Well-Fed Friends by Nonny Hogrogian
Billy Goat doesn't want to end up as the Farmer's supper…

The Pearl by Helme Heine
Beaver realises that there are greater riches in life than even the loveliest of pearls.

If I Had … by Mercer Mayer
'If only I had a gorilla, a crocodile, a snake … then no one would pick on me!' A little boy's daydreams find a real-life answer.

King Rooster, Queen Hen by Anita Lobel
Rooster and Hen set out to be King and Queen in the big city, but meet crafty Fox, with almost disastrous results …

Bill and Stanley by Helen Oxenbury
A busy afternoon for Bill and his best friend, the mildly eccentric dog Stanley.

Santa's Crash–Bang Christmas
by Steven Kroll and Tomie de Paola
A very clumsy Father Christmas brings havoc to a peaceful house.

Hurry Home, Grandma!
by Arielle North Olson and Lydia Dabcovich
Will Grandma, the dauntless explorer, make it home from the jungle in time to help decorate the Christmas tree?

The Bear's Bicycle by Emilie Warren McLeod and David McPhail
The hair-raising adventures of the bumbling bear make a funny introduction to the rules of road safety.

Tough Eddie by Elizabeth Winthrop and Lillian Hoban
There is more to tough-guy Eddie than meets the eye …